RICHARD
GOES
SAILING

BY JANET DUCHESNE

DELACORTE PRESS · NEW YORK

It was Saturday, so Richard was not at school. He had nobody to play with. Johnny-next-door was away. Willy, the spotted dog, was busy chewing a bone—too busy to play with Richard.

"What shall I do?" Richard asked Mother.

"Go out in the garden and play," said Mother.

So Richard went into the garden and swung on the swing. He swung for quite a long time.

I wonder what I shall do after this? he thought.

Suddenly he heard the telephone begin to ring indoors. Mother answered it long before he could stop the swing and get down, and by the time he had run up the garden and through the house she had nearly finished talking.

"Eleven o'clock, then," she said. "We'll be there. Thank you very much. Goodbye!"

"Who was that?" asked Richard.

"Ah-ha," said Mother.

"Where are we going, then?" asked Richard.

"Ah-ha to that, too," said Mother. "I'll go and tell your father to get the car out."

Mother put fruit and biscuits and cheese in the car.

"Are we going for a picnic?" asked Richard.

"Not exactly," said Father.

"Is Willy coming?" asked Richard.

"No," said Father.

"We can't be going to the seaside, then," said Richard.

"Are we going to the Museum?" he asked.

He knew dogs were not allowed in the Museum.

"No, we're not," said Mother. "Just you wait and see!"

So they said "Goodbye" to Willy and started off. It was half past nine.

"It must be a long way to Where-ever-it-is," said Richard.

Mother read the map and told Father which turnings to take. The country was hilly at first, then flatter and flatter. They went through three towns, and so many villages that Richard lost count.

At ten to eleven Mother said, "Turn right here, after the bridge. Only half a mile to go."

They went along a narrow road beside a river. Soon Father stopped the car outside some big wooden buildings. There were boats everywhere, in the river and on shore.

Mother and Father and Richard climbed out of the car just as three other people came round the corner of a shed to meet them.

"It's Mr and Mrs Price and Sandra!" cried Richard.

"Now can you guess what we're going to do today?" asked Father.

Richard knew that Mr Price had an old boat and that he had worked on it in his garden until it was as good as new again.

"Is Mr Price's boat here?" he asked. "Are we going sailing in it?"

"Right first guess," said Father.

"Hello, Sandra!" shouted Richard. "We're coming sailing in your boat!"

Mr Price's boat was called *Polly*. She was
waiting at the end of a jetty. Annabel, Sandra's
Siamese cat, was waiting, too. Now Richard
knew why Willy had to stay at home . . . Annabel was not friendly with dogs.

Everybody went on board.

Sandra and Richard both put on life-jackets in case they fell in.

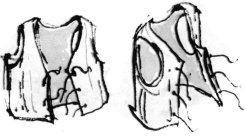

The first thing Mrs Price did was to put the kettle on. There was a real gas-stove. It had an oven, and two gas-rings with a little railing round them in case things fell off when the boat heeled over.

The grown-ups had coffee in striped mugs.

Sandra had milk, and Richard had lemonade.

"Let's start now," said Mr Price. "Then there will be time for a good long sail before we bring you back. You want to be home in time for supper, don't you?"

Father said, "Yes."

Then Mr Price and Father got the sails up.

Sandra cast off the rope that kept *Polly* close to the jetty, and jumped back on board at the last minute. Richard helped to push out into the river, and they were off!

Annabel sat just inside the cabin and watched.

They went past big ships and little boats,

fast boats and slow ones,

processions of swans

cows, trees and bungalows

and an enormous power-station pouring out

clouds of smoke.

They were going downstream, towards the sea. Now the river was wider, and there were fewer boats. Mr Price let Sandra steer and Richard looked carefully to see what she did.

When she wanted the *Polly* to go to the right, she pushed the tiller to the left. When she wanted her to go to the left, she pushed the tiller to the right.

POLLY

After Sandra, everyone else had a turn.

Father said it would take him a long time to learn how to steer a boat, because he was used to driving the car and turning the wheel the way he wanted to go, and not the way he didn't want to go!

Mother laughed. "Don't start thinking you're in the car today," she said, "or you'll have us aground."

Soon it was time for lunch. They stopped by a little island and tied the *Polly* to two trees. Then they all got out and sat on the green grassy bank to have the picnic.

They had cold meat and tomatoes, and bread and butter, and Mother's fruit and biscuits and cheese. There was more coffee and lemonade, and chocolate to finish up with. Annabel had a saucer of milk.

After lunch Richard and Sandra explored the island. Richard climbed a tree. Sandra picked some flowers and found an empty bottle to put them in.

They watched a man fishing, but he did not catch anything.

Mother did the washing-up in the *Polly* and Sandra and Richard helped. When they finished it was time to set sail again.

Round the next bend, the river was very wide, so wide that the banks were almost out of sight. Richard felt as if they must be out at sea.

"We mustn't go any farther," said Mr Price. "The tide will be against us on the way back, so it will take longer."

He swung the boat round.

"Who wants a turn now?" he asked.

"I do, please!" said Father, and changed places with Mr Price.

Richard was sitting by the mast, being look-out.

"There's a little island over there," he said presently, pointing.

"It's a sandbank," said Sandra.

"That means there is shallow water here and we must be careful," said Mr Price. "Better move out towards the middle of the river."

Father moved the tiller a little, and they changed course.

"Now, everybody," said Mr Price, "keep your eyes open!"

All at once Richard called out, "There's one, nearly in front of us!"

"Turn left, quickly!" said Mr Price to Father.

But . . . oh dear! Father forgot that he was in a boat, not in a car. He pushed the tiller to the left, hard, and the *Polly* shot round to the right, straight at the sandbank.

"The other way!" shouted Mr Price but it was too late.

There was a soft, bumpy feeling under the boat, and a jerk. Everyone held on to something, except Sandra, who sat down suddenly. Richard held on to the mast. Annabel held on to Mr Price's trouser-leg with all her claws, and he said, "Ouch!"

With one last bump, the boat stopped moving.

"We're aground!" said Mother.

"I am most awfully sorry," said Father.

Quickly, they took the sails down. Then they all went as far to the stern end of the boat as they could, and tried to rock the *Polly* off the sand . . . but nothing happened.

Then Mr Price started the engine and put it in reverse. It spluttered and roared, and the propeller churned up a lot of mud. But the boat stayed still.

"What can we do now? We seem to be stuck,"
said Richard.

"Nothing," said Mr Price. "We'll have to
wait until the tide comes up again and floats us
off, and that won't happen until about three
hours from now."

Three hours sounded a very long time.

"We'll be late for supper," said Richard.
"Willy will wonder what has happened to us."

"Poor Willy," said Mother.

The sandbank began to grow bigger and bigger as the tide ran out.

The *Polly* heeled over more

and more

and more, until she was almost lying on her side.

There was nothing flat to walk on or sit on.

Richard thought it felt very funny.

Mrs Price thought it felt funny, too, when she tried to make tea in a sloping place.

The seagulls overhead sounded as if they were laughing.

"It's all very well for you," said Mr Price to the seagulls.

There was sand all round the *Polly* now, instead of water. Mr Price hung a ladder over the side and Richard and Sandra climbed down. They took some biscuits. Annabel went too.

"Let's play we're shipwrecked sailors," said Sandra.

"Let's pretend the biscuits are coconuts," said Richard. "We must stay here for years and years, waiting to be rescued."

They made a white flag out of a handkerchief and a stick, and put it in the middle of the island for rescuers to see.

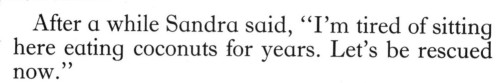

After a while Sandra said, "I'm tired of sitting here eating coconuts for years. Let's be rescued now."

She fetched the white flag and waved it.

"Somebody has seen us," said Richard.

Mr Price was coming down the ladder. "You must come on board again," he said. "The water has begun to rise and we don't want you to be cut off."

The island was shrinking. Already, there was some water between it and the boat. Mr Price picked up the shipwrecked sailors and put them on the deck. Then he climbed in himself, pulled up the ladder, and put it away.

"Thank you for rescuing us, Daddy," said Sandra.

"Now we all need rescuing," said Richard. "Let's wave the flag again."

Other boats went by. The people in them smiled and waved back when they saw the flag.

One person laughed and shouted at them. "Are you stuck?" he cried.

"Shall we be stuck much longer?" asked Richard.

"Not much longer now," said Mr Price.

"I think we're beginning to move," said Richard hopefully.

"I think the boat is standing up straighter, anyway," said Sandra.

Just then a powerful motor-boat came along. It slowed down, and turned in a circle. Finally it stopped quite close to the *Polly*. The man in it looked friendly.

"Good afternoon, Mr Price," he called. "Can I give you any help?"

"It's Jim who works at the boatyard!" said Sandra.

"Thank you, Jim!" called Mr Price. "We're very glad to see you!"

Jim and Mr Price fastened a long rope between the two boats. Jim started his engine. The rope tightened, and the motor-boat pulled and pulled.

"We're moving now!" shouted Richard.

He was right. The *Polly* came sliding off the sand . . . and rocked . . . and stood up straight. She was floating again at last.

"Hooray!" they all shouted at once and Annabel gave a loud *Miaow*.

"Are you in a hurry to get back?" Jim asked.
"Yes, we are, rather," said Mr Price.
"I'll tow you all the way, then," said Jim.

So the *Polly* started for home behind Jim's powerful motor-boat.

In next to no time, it seemed to Richard, he and
Mother and Father were saying goodbye to the
others and climbing into the car.

"Come again another day," said Sandra.

"I'll try to steer properly next time," called
Father as they drove away.

The car journey seemed even quicker than the boat trip because Richard went to sleep. When he woke up they were at home.

Willy was barking and barking because he was so pleased to see them.

And they were not so very late for supper after all.